The

Shepherd

The
Shepherd

Alfred Wurr

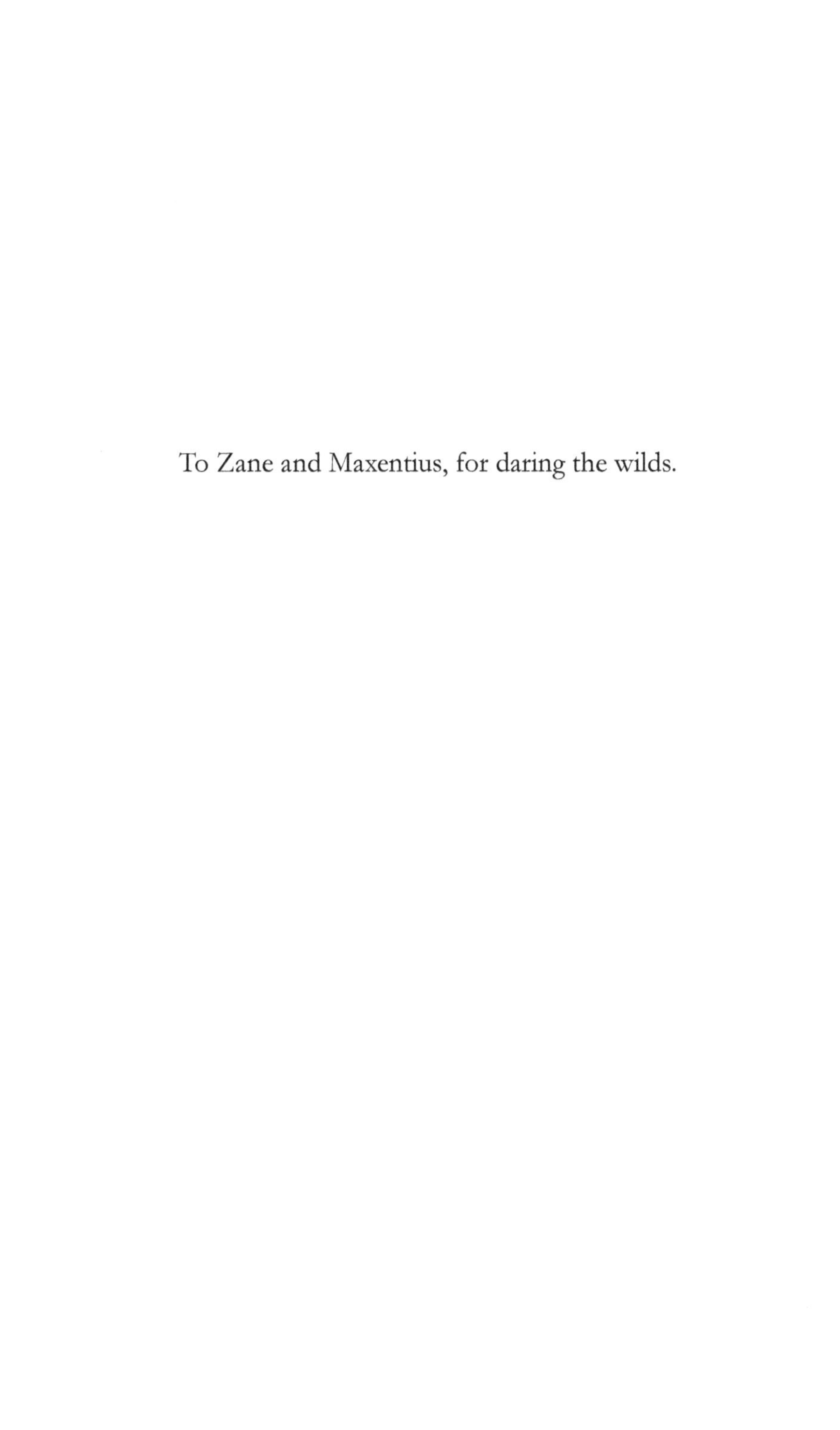

To Zane and Maxentius, for daring the wilds.

Contents

Welcome

In case you don't know, *The Shepherd* tells the story of what happens to Alan, Brad, Lilith, and Lucy after the events of *Phantom Frost*.

Accordingly, if you haven't yet read *Phantom Frost*, I recommend reading it first. Reading *The Shepherd* first won't ruin *Phantom Frost*, but there are a few unavoidable spoilers, so you may want to take that into consideration.

Whatever order you read the series, thank you for supporting my work. Your patronage makes these books possible.

The

Shepherd

Chapter 1

Brad

Before he fully knew why, Brad shuffled right and peered past the window's edge at the white box truck in the street. Large letters across the vehicle's side marked it as a moving truck rental. A common sight in his neighbourhood, but something about it still gave him pause.

He thought back over the past few days.

He'd seen it before. Hadn't he?

He turned and rushed for his desk, passing his girlfriend, Lucy, asleep on the bed. She lay on her stomach, one naked leg poking from beneath the sheets, her head buried beneath a pillow against the morning light. Despite the urgency, his eyes traced the smoothness of her exposed leg up the curve of her thigh to her shapely, sheet-clad bottom. Pulling the top drawer of the small desk open with a squeak, he pawed the contents, pushing aside pens, paper clips and a stapler, before his fingers closed on a pair of binoculars.

Lucy murmured in her sleep as he slunk back to the window. Standing at the edge of the rectangle of sunlight that crept across the hardwood, he held the field glasses up to his eyes. A dog barked as Brad panned the street, trying to align the eyepieces with the vehicle.

A smudge of black and white came into view, and he reached up to adjust the dials.

"Hey," Lucy mumbled from the bed. "Nice cheeks . . . but maybe you should put on some pants. The neighbours are going to get an eyeful."

A rush of warmth came to his face. "No chance; the sun's too bright right now," he said, still looking through the binoculars. "The only thing anyone's going to see is sun glare."

"Well, come back to bed anyway," Lucy said, patting the sheets. "I'm freezing . . . and it's been weeks since we've had a morning alone, together."

She had a point. They'd spent the past three weeks chauffeuring his younger brother, Alan, Alan's girlfriend, Lilith, and Alan's best buddy, Caleb, around Utah and Nevada. With Lilith sleeping above them in the crawlspace of his Volkswagen van, they had had little time to themselves. It had gotten even worse once they'd met Shivurr. Being kidnapped by government agents was a real mood killer.

They had pulled back into town late the previous night. After dropping Lilith at home and Alan at his parents' place, they'd returned to their apartment. With the fridge empty and hungry from the road, they'd ordered pizza, devoured it, showered, and made up for lost time before falling into a deep sleep. That was, until the sun rose.

He'd have liked nothing better than to hop back into bed next to her, feel the warmth and smoothness of her supple body and make up for lost time, again, but first he had to be sure they were still safe.

His stomach twisted as the image crystallized. Barely perceptible, even with binoculars, he spotted a dent in the side of the truck—an impression left by Alan's elbow less than forty-eight hours before.

A brave but pointless act of defiance. His kid brother had a temper.

Brad swore. *It's got to be them*. He hadn't noticed the

signage on the truck's side when they'd been taken, but the damage to the side panel clinched it.

Less than two days since Shivurr had broken them out, the Bodhi Group had found them, again.

They should have known. They hadn't told their captors their names, and in their haste, the agents hadn't gotten their IDs, but that wasn't going to protect his and his friends' identities for long. Finding out Brad's address from the licence plate on his van, or checking with the hotel in Tonopah where they'd first been questioned by Bodhi Group agents (pretending to be FBI), would have been child's play for such an organization.

He supposed he'd known it, deep down, but he'd hoped that the Group would have bigger problems to deal with after what had happened at the Institute. Even if the mostly subterranean facility wasn't ashes by now, Brad had reasoned that with Shivurr now beyond their reach and the legality of their actions questionable, the Bodhi Group would choose to leave them alone. Just in case, he had planned to discuss what to do next with his parents. Perhaps they'd engage a lawyer or get the FBI involved or maybe the papers, but they couldn't do that if they were taken again.

Slender arms wrapped around his waist, giving him a squeeze.

"Something wrong?" Lucy asked.

The doors of the truck opened, and four men spilled out onto the street.

Brad lowered the binoculars and turned to Lucy, who looked up at him with a smile, her long, wavy blond hair tousled from sleep. *Like an adorable punk rocker.* "Get dressed." He raced for the nearby chest of drawers. "Hurry. They're here."

"What? Who's here?"

Brad danced from one leg to the other, pulling on fresh underwear. "Agents . . . the Group. They're heading for the building."

Lucy's eyes widened. "What? But . . . they can't . . . it's not fair. We can't help them anymore. Shivurr's gone."

"I know, Luce," Brad said. "But they don't know that. We've got to get out of here. C'mon, get dressed."

Lucy raced to the bedroom's only chair, where her clothes sat in a pile. Flinging her pants to the side, she located and pulled on undergarments before slipping her head through the neck of the T-shirt she'd worn the night before.

Brad zipped up his pants as the front-door intercom buzzed. The young couple looked at each other, faces tense, but continued to dress. He grabbed a fresh T-shirt from a drawer and pulled it on. He held out a hand to Lucy as she hiked up her jeans and buttoned the fly, and they fled into the living room, heading for the door leading to the hallway.

Brad grabbed his wallet and keys from the table as the buzzer squawked a second time by his ear. He grasped the doorknob, holding his other hand against the frame.

"Brad, wait," Lucy said, strapping her purse across her chest bandolier-style. "That's got to be them. I'll let them in."

"Are you serious? Why?"

"So we can go down the back stairs while they come up. It may buy us time."

He looked at her for a long moment, then nodded. "Go for it."

She held an index finger to her lips and pressed the button to talk. "Hello. Who is it?"

"Hi there," said a deep voice in a friendly tone. "Would you buzz me in? I got locked out."

Brad opened the door to the hallway, stepping to the side to clear the path for Lucy.

She nodded to him, then pressed the transmit button. "Come on in," she said, punching the button to open the door.

Without waiting for a reply, she slipped into the hallway. Brad pulled the door shut and turned the deadbolt to the locked position with a thunk. Together, the couple fled for the back stairs as a staccato of footsteps echoed from the front stairwell.

Chapter 2

Alan

Alan squeezed his eyes tight against the warm orange glow of the rising sun. The ocean swelled and dipped, hiding the beach behind a froth of white water. The wide strip of sand came back into view a moment later. Garbage cans and lifeguard towers stood sentinel at regular intervals, connected by tire tracks in the sand.

It felt good to be home. Back on his board, riding the waves. Already, the past week felt unreal, like a dream he'd had after taking a puff of one of Caleb's joints.

Except, it wasn't. Lilith, Caleb, Alan's brother, Brad, and Brad's girlfriend, Lucy, had shared in it.

Turns out the world's a lot more radical than most people know.

The call of other members of the Dawn Patrol rose above the sea's endless susurration, signalling the approach of a surfable swell. He caught the wave with practised ease and smiled. His time away from the ocean hadn't dulled his skills.

He ducked lower as the wave curled, moving him inexorably toward the beach.

If their shared experience wasn't enough to prove it wasn't a dream, there was also the fact that Caleb was still out there, somewhere.

According to Shivurr, Alan's lifelong friend now surfed waves somewhere on the shores of a Pacific Ocean paradise. Surfed with beings once worshipped as gods in

Ancient Greece and who knew where else. Alan had seen enough to believe it all without too much hesitation. There isn't any story a living snowman could tell you that wouldn't seem plausible, given the source.

Not that they'd be able to tell anyone, least of all their parents. No way their parents would believe it, and if they did, they'd totally freak. Brad lived on his own, but Alan wouldn't be able to leave the house until he was eighteen if his folks knew what they'd been through. Yet he knew that his brother still wanted to try. To concoct some version of the story that they'd swallow, so that they could figure out a plan to protect themselves from the Group. What that story would be, Alan couldn't imagine.

Brad had told him to say nothing until he'd had time to think about it.

Alan was happy to oblige.

He rode the wave's crest to the shallows, pushing aside feelings of envy. Surfing bitchin' waves with gods on fresh shores, somewhere, would be awesome beyond belief. He should've gone with Shivurr and Scott after the fire at the Schmidts'. Maybe then he'd be doing the same. He hopped off his surfboard and dunked his head beneath the water before popping up. He threw his head back to get his long hair out of his eyes.

Envy aside, he missed his bro and hoped he'd soon be back. School was less than a month away. Caleb wasn't the best student and starting late wasn't going to help.

Alan tucked his board under an arm and sloshed through the surf onto the beach. Sticking it into the sand, he sat on the large towel he'd brought and watched the water.

Going back to school after summer sucked, normally. He'd always rather be surfing, but after what he'd experienced, returning to the tedium of a classroom appealed even less than usual. He'd have to make the most of what remained of the summer. That bodacious babe, Olivia, and that Wilhelm dude were going to bring Caleb back soon. Once they did, he'd try to convince Brad to drive them all up to Big Sur for a few days before summer's end. Surfing locally was choice, but he could always do that on weekends after school started. Besides, it might not be a bad idea to bounce for a bit in case those Bodhi Group dudes came looking for them again.

If any survived.

Content with his plan, he pulled on a pair of sunglasses and stretched out his legs. He leaned back onto his elbows, giving his long hair a chance to drip dry in the sun. His eyes roamed left to the stretch of sand extending into the distance, then panned right, lingering on ships far out on the water backed by the dark outlines of large islands, then further right to the pier. Standing on thick pillars, thirty feet above, a wide pier stretched southwest, a few thousand feet straight out into the water. A bridge to nowhere with a large tower halfway down its length from which rescuers watched over the beach. As he did so, a large bird with a dark body and crimson head leaped from the iron railing that bordered the pier's walkway. Held aloft by six-foot-wide wings of black, tipped with feathers of light grey, it soared above the surf, then dipped toward town.

Alan turned his head to the left, following the bird until it ranged out of his field of view, then turned back to the water.

A turkey vulture, he thought. *Must be a dead fish nearby.* His mind roamed back to the previous day. *Just like the bird Bear chased at Dublin Gulch.*

He'd never given them much thought before. Like species of trees or types of grass or people he didn't know, they were just part of the background until they got right up in your face. Thinking back, he'd often seen the birds picking at carcasses by the roadside.

Ooglay as fuck too. Must be why Bear hates them. He snorted. *But what else should they look like? It'd be weird if they were cute.* He smiled, imagining a bunch of bunnies feeding on carrion.

Yawning, Alan lay flat and closed his eyes.

They'd arrived home pretty late, and he'd gotten up early, eager to get back to the beach. He inhaled deeply, savouring the salty sea air.

Time to catch a few Zs, he thought as he fell asleep, listening to the shouts of surfers and crash of waves, still smiling.

Chapter 3

Lilith

Lilith hiked her surfboard higher as she crossed the street. She'd walked several blocks already, and her biceps burned, despite repeatedly shifting her cargo from one arm to the other. Walking west, down Main Street, she passed the ice cream shop where she sometimes worked for extra cash. She'd have to stop in on her way home, get back on the schedule now that they'd returned from vacation.

Later, though.

She wanted to get some surfing in first and hang out with Alan. She knew he'd be on the beach now. He'd said as much, and he spent every moment he could surfing, preparing for the competitions that were so important to him. She didn't mind. Surfing was how they'd met. Though a skilled skateboarder, Lilith had somehow never learned to surf until about a year ago. Alan taught surfing for spending money, and she'd taken one of his group classes to get started.

With her skateboarding background, she'd been his best student by far. They'd had an immediate connection and soon they were getting serious. Good thing, too. If she didn't surf, they'd spend a lot less time together. Though he could be a bit clueless and spent too much time with Caleb, playing arcade games (she liked them too but didn't want to play them quite as often), he was also kind and funny . . . not to mention gorgeous. Most of all, she felt safe with him, like he'd never hurt her or allow her to be hurt.

She felt a pang of regret, thinking back to how she'd treated him after Lunar Crater. It hadn't been fair. Lucy had later told her how Alan had looked ready to charge the creep with the gun.

The one that had stared at her with that pervy leer. It made her sick to think about what might have happened.

Alan had been ready to risk his life. *For me.* Yet she'd made him feel like he'd failed her. *Am I a horrible person?* She'd just been so scared . . . and angry, even days later. But she shouldn't have taken it out on him.

She swiped at her eyes and sucked in a breath of air. *Stop it, Lilith*, she thought. *We made up. It's old news.*

They were all safe. Thanks to Shivurr. Their saviour of ice and snow. An unlikely hero, but one for whom she felt great affection—not just because he'd defended them repeatedly, but for the caring and gentle soul that he'd proven to be. A cool dude, as Alan liked to say, literally and figuratively. Full of curiosity for life's wonders and sincere in his treatment of them all.

If he hadn't been there . . . they could all be lying dead in the desert for all she knew. Almost certainly, she wouldn't be about to go surfing with her boyfriend now. She might be at Alan's funeral at the very least. The snowman had saved them all, but he had also needed saving, and they'd done what they could. If things had gone according to plan, he should now be safe on an island somewhere in the Pacific Ocean. She hoped it was enough but knew that it wasn't.

It almost seemed like a dream now. *Insane, really.* Except that they'd all shared in it. *Are we all crazy?* She didn't think so. Her Wiccan aunt, a practising psychic, had fostered in her a faith in the preternatural. If you accepted the existence of ghosts and witchcraft, you had to allow for the possibility of other wondrous things. *Don't you?*

She pushed aside such thoughts as she crossed to the beach side of the highway. Taking a stairwell that ran alongside the pier, she descended to beach level. She turned left onto a path that ran parallel to the water, heading for their usual place.

She spotted Alan out on the sand as she did so. He walked just off to her right, heading in the direction of the parking lot that lay just beyond the restaurant to her left, about a hundred feet away.

Alan's head spun left at Lilith's call, and she waved an arm. After a long moment, he waved back, then turned to the woman at his side. The redhead nodded in Lilith's direction, lips moving. Seconds later, Alan rotated and jogged toward Lilith, leaving the woman behind.

Brushing strands of hair out of her eyes, Lilith walked to meet him.

Chapter 4

Brad

Reaching ground level, the couple slipped out the rear entrance. Brad eased the door shut, then rushed toward his Volkswagen van, Otto the Autobus. It sat tucked into a stall in the small parking lot reserved for residents.

Brad readied his keys as he jogged, nearly dropping them in his haste. With a quick tug, he opened the passenger-side door for Lucy. Without waiting, he ran to the driver's side and climbed inside. Before long, he steered toward the lot's exit and took an immediate left.

Pulling out onto the street at the front of the building, he accelerated.

As they neared the box truck, he downshifted, then pressed the brake.

"Why are you stopping?" Lucy asked.

"That's their truck," he replied.

She narrowed an eye, twisting her lips.

Brad cocked an eyebrow and tilted his head down, looking toward the vehicle's tires.

Her eyes brightened and she smiled as he slipped into the back seat.

"Great idea," she said, looking back at the front door of their apartment block. "Hurry, though."

Loose clothes and camping equipment flew as he rummaged around.

"Aha," Brad said, unfolding a knife with a three-inch blade.

"Okay, go." Lucy shimmied sideways toward the driver's seat. "I'll keep the car running. *Andale.*"

"*Arriba, arriba,*" he replied, exiting via the van's large side door. "Let me know if you see them coming."

He left it ajar as he ran to the first tire and stabbed its sidewall. Warm compressed air burst from the rubber, and the truck wobbled as it sank.

Sidling right, he thrust the knife a second time. The blade slipped, raising a well of blood from his palm, but the tire still collapsed.

As the truck sank onto its rims, he contemplated leaving the last two wheels intact. *Even Otto should be fast enough to outrun a large truck with two flat tires.*

"Brad," Lucy yelled. "They're coming."

That settles it. Turning, he bounded for the gaping side door and plunged inside. Whirling as he entered, he slid the door shut, slamming it into place with practised ease.

"Whoa!" Brad's arms flailed as the vehicle surged forward, sending him rolling toward the back.

"Sorry, sweetie," Lucy said.

"Don't sweat it, babe." Brad braced himself against the back seat with a forearm. He clambered awkwardly onto the bench as blood continued to well from his hand. With his palm pressed to his lips, he looked out the rear window as the bark of a dog broke the morning's calm.

The same four men he had seen from his apartment window now stood by the building's entrance with their backs to him.

"What are they looking at?" Brad asked.

The dog's throaty and penetrating bark grew louder.

"Dunno," Lucy replied, "but—"

A blur of black-and-white fur emerged from behind a

parked car, heading straight for the milling agents.

Brad narrowed his eyes and his mouth gaped. *No . . . way.* He whirled in his seat as the van shifted to the left and scrambled to the side window. With his face pressed to the glass, he watched as one of the agents knelt to pet a large black-and-white dog, tail wagging.

"Bear?" he said under his breath.

A house rushed in from Brad's left, cutting off his view of the scene.

"What's that, sweetie?"

"Wilhelm's dog." He moved to the front, using the ceiling to steady himself against the sway of the vehicle. "You heard that bark, right?"

"Are you sure?"

"Not really . . . no. Sure looked like him, though."

"What about the agents? Did they see us?"

"No, I don't think so." He snatched tissues from the box he kept on the dash. "Bear . . . or whatever dog it was distracted them."

"How could it be him? We left him with Shivurr at Dublin Gulch. That's hours away . . . by car."

"I know," Brad said. He wiped blood from his palm with a tissue, then pressed it against the wound. "Must have been another Alaskan shepherd."

Movement in his peripheral vision drew his eye to the side mirror.

"Slow down, Luce."

"Huh?" Lucy took her foot off the gas. "What's wrong?"

"That dog's chasing us." He reached for the door latch. "Stop, stop, stop. It's him. It's him."

Lucy pushed the brake, bringing the vehicle to a crawl and then a halt.

Brad threw his door wide. "Here, Bear." The dog leaped

up, through the opening, slathering Brad's chin and nose with saliva. "Whoa." He chortled. "Easy now."

"Is it really him?" Lucy asked.

"Yeah," Brad replied. "I'd know this furry guy anywhere."

"Well, he sure seems to recognize us," Lucy said.

"Oh, it's him all right. Look at the pattern of his fur. It's him."

Sharp claws dug into Brad's thighs as the Alaskan shepherd's nose pushed toward Lucy. Scooping a hand under the dog's hindquarters, Brad pulled him inside. He wiped his face and reached for the open door as Lucy squealed.

"All right," Lucy said. "All right. Ugh. Yes, yes. We love you too."

"C'mon, Bear." Brad gave the dog a gentle shove toward the vehicle's rear. "C'mon. Get in the back."

To Brad's surprise, the dog wriggled into the back in apparent obedience. A thick tail batted their shoulders as their furry companion slipped by. Bear circled the back, sniffing surfaces, before returning. He placed his head between the two humans and barked.

"We should go," Lucy said, pressing the clutch to the floor.

"Good idea," Brad replied, rubbing Bear's head.

"We need to find Lilith and Alan. Agents are probably looking for them too."

Brad checked his watch. "Swing by the pier. Alan's probably there."

"This early?"

"Yeah," Brad said. "He was pretty stoked to get back to the beach."

"And Lilith?"

"Dunno. If she's not, we'll check her house after. It's not all that far from the beach anyway."

Lucy glanced at Bear. "How do you think he found us?"

"Not sure." He looked out the window. "Maybe Shivurr's with him."

"You don't think he made it home?"

"I don't know, Luce." Brad shrugged. "He's a resilient dude. Yeah . . . I think he made it." He rubbed Bear's head. The dog snuffled his shoulder in return. "Doesn't explain how this guy found us, though."

"Maybe he tracked us. You know, with his nose."

Brad glanced at her. "You think?"

"I've heard of dogs journeying thousands of miles to get home."

"Sure, but over two hundred in a night?"

"Who knows?" Lucy tossed her shoulders. "He keeps company with gods. He's got to be a pretty special dog, right?"

Chapter 5

Alan

Alan opened his eyes sometime later, unsure what had awakened him, but glad for it. His nap had been fitful, filled with creatures of fire that pursued him across the waves to a shoreline that he could never seem to reach. A shoreline where a woman with long red hair beckoned, her six-foot-long tresses flowing about her shoulders like a cape. She never spoke a word until the end, when at last she said—

"Excuse me," said a feminine voice.

Oh, right, he thought. *Not part of the dream.*

Alan sat up, eyes slits, holding a hand to his face to block the light. The sky had clouded over, but he still felt like a vampire at high noon despite his sunglasses. The air had warmed a few degrees too.

Must have been out a while.

He pulled himself to his feet, rubbing his face, and regarded the speaker.

"Are you Alan?" His eyes snapped wide as the newcomer, a twenty-something babe, came into focus: five-foot-four with shoulder-length red hair, a gorgeous face shaded by a floppy wide-brimmed hat, and a bodacious bod.

Alan could only stare in reply.

"The surfing instructor?" the woman continued, a faint accent to her voice. "I've never surfed before." She smiled and pointed to his surfboard. "I thought perhaps you'd teach me. I'd be happy to pay you."

"I like your accent," he said, trying his best to maintain eye contact. "Are you from Germany?"

"Yes. I'm visiting from Berlin."

"West or East?" Alan grinned.

The girl cocked an eyebrow. "Most definitely the East."

"As if." He chuckled. "How'd you make it past the wall? Tunnel or hot air balloon?"

"Private jet, actually."

"Righteous." *Girl likes to play.* "What's your name? Heidi?"

"You may call me Greta."

"Pleased to meet you," Alan said, holding out a hand. She clasped it and squeezed, hard. *Strong grip.* "How'd you know I teach surfing?"

"Some boys over there," she said, glancing to her right.

Alan didn't look, unable to tear his eyes from her body. *The dude that invented sunglasses is a freaking genius.*

He eyed her ivory skin, devoid of tan lines, skin white as snow, not a freckle in sight. *Never surfed before? No shit,* he thought. He'd not met a local who didn't have a suntan of some sort, even if just face or forearms. *I hope she's wearing major sunscreen, even if it is cloudy.*

"I would really like to learn." She turned her back to him to regard the water. "This is my first time to the ocean."

Alan's eyes roved down her back. He stifled a gasp and bugged his eyes. *Oh god.* A line of sky-blue fabric rose from between two shapely round cheeks before flaring out to each hip.

East meets West, he thought. *Together, the best.* Alan's regrets over having missed his chance to surf with gods diminished. *This is so much better.*

He coughed and wrenched his neck upward as she rotated to face him. *Is it hot out here?* He squatted and snatched his towel from the sand. Springing erect, he dabbed the terrycloth against a cheek, then held it taut at his waist.

"Will you?" she asked, saying the first word as if it began with the letter V.

He considered a moment.

If Lilith saw him with her, she'd probably wig out, but it'd be rude to refuse. Holding the woman's hotness against her didn't seem right. She probably had to put up with that sort of bigotry all the time, which was hardly fair . . . and she was a tourist. Tourism supported the local economy. He had a civic duty to be friendly. Didn't he? Besides, a bit of extra cash was always welcome.

"Uh . . . yeah," Alan mumbled. "Shh . . . sure," he said, forgetting to negotiate a price.

"Would you mind helping me with my surfboard?" She looked toward the parking lot that bordered the beach. "I left it at the car. It is quite heavy . . ."

Alan stood taller. "Of course." He turned to his left and cupped his hands to the sides of his mouth. "Yo, Harry."

Harry Chen, a dark-haired classmate and fellow surfer, about Alan's age, turned at Alan's call.

"S'up, Davis?" Harry replied, using Alan's last name.

"Mind watching my stuff? I'll be back in five."

"No worries, dude," replied Harry.

"Thanks, bro." Alan looked back to Greta and gestured with a hand. "Lead the way."

She smirked and raised a brow, then moved toward the distant vehicles.

Alan watched her go a moment.

He shook his head. *All right, dude.* He took a deep breath. *You've got a freaking girlfriend.*

He raced to catch up, taking one last long look at his

new student's pert bottom.

As he neared, a flash of yellow near the middle of her back caught his eye. He snorted as he recognized it.

Forgot to take off the price tag, he thought, noting the yellow tag trapped against her body beneath the strap, still fastened by a piece of string, as he fell in alongside her. *No one's perfect, I guess.*

He started to wonder about the wisdom of agreeing to give Greta surfing lessons.

Is this a pickup? He imagined adults hooked up all the time. Without parents to hold you back and a place of your own, people over eighteen must be doing it all the freaking time. *It's a wonder they ever leave the house.*

A part of him hungered at the thought of what could happen, but if he ever hurt Lilith, he'd have to kick his own ass. He loved her, even if she made his life . . . difficult, sometimes.

"I have a girlfriend," Alan said as they walked.

There, got that out of the way. He wasn't hiding anything and had no plans to make any moves. *She's got to be at least five years older anyway.* No chance she'd be looking to score with a teenager. Sure, people told him he looked a bit older than his sixteen years, maybe even eighteen or nineteen, but there was still no way. In any case, he wasn't and wouldn't do anything, even if there was—no one could accuse him of not being a good guy.

Sure, this Greta chick is one Schweet Betty, but so's Lil. He swallowed, imagining Lilith wearing a swimsuit like Greta's. *Hotter, even.*

The woman looked back and chuckled. "How very nice for you." She put a hand on his shoulder. "She's a lucky girl."

He blushed. "Uh, thanks."

"Alan," shouted a voice from his left.

A waving arm ahead and to his left drew his attention. Alan flushed a deeper red and returned Lilith's wave.

Oh, man. He swivelled to regard his new surfing student. "Uh, just a second, uh . . . Greta. That's my girl."

"Oh, how perfect," Greta said. "She's lovely."

"I just got to say hello."

"Of course you do." Greta shooed him with a hand. "Go right ahead. I will catch up."

Chapter 6

Lilith

Clumps of sand kicked up behind him as Alan jogged closer. Ten feet from her, he pulled to a stop, flicked his hair out of his eyes, and smiled. He reached up and tugged his sunglasses down and toward the tip of his nose, then winked.

"Hey, Lil."

"Who's that?" Lilith asked, looking past his shoulder.

"Huh? Oh, uh, a new surfing student."

"She's beautiful," Lilith said.

"Uh, yeah, I suppose so."

Lilith rolled her eyes.

"Want me to carry your surfboard?" Alan asked.

"Sure, thanks."

She stood it on its tail and held it out to him.

He grabbed it, tucking it under an arm, then turned sideways, draping a muscled arm across her shoulders. He smelled of coconut and sweat. She squeezed him back and peered past his chest at the scantily clad woman, still thirty feet away. Lilith squinted, thinking about the T-shirt and neon board shorts that she wore.

"Why are so many of your students gorgeous?"

The redhead stopped, turned right, and fixed her eyes on the parking lot. Lilith frowned, noting bare side boob extending past the woman's left shoulder. Her eyes roved over the woman's curvy form, popping wide as they reached her bottom.

"Oh my god," Lilith said. "Where's the rest of her bathing suit? You can totally see her—"

The woman pivoted and strode toward them, flashing a broad white smile.

Lilith tucked an errant lock of hair behind an ear, wishing she'd left her hair down rather than tying it back in a ponytail. She felt prettiest that way.

Doesn't matter. Alan liked her updo just as much; he'd said so often enough.

"Hey, Greta," Alan said as the woman neared. "This is my girl, Lilith. Lil, this is Greta." He smiled. "She's here from Germany."

A silver bracelet glinted in the sunlight as the woman held out a hand. "Very nice to meet you."

Lilith stared, eyeing the woman's chiclet-white teeth. "Hi," she said after a long moment, taking the offered hand. Remembering her manners, she continued, "Nice to meet you too."

Greta fingered the ruby pendant hanging about her neck. She flicked her eyes to Alan, then back to Lilith. "Alan has agreed to instruct me in surfing. I see that you are yourself a surfer, yes?"

"She's wicked," Alan said, giving Lilith's shoulders a short squeeze. "My best student."

"How wonderful," Greta replied, still looking at Lilith. "I hope to do half as well." She cast her eyes to Alan, then right to regard the parking lot. "Shall we?"

"For sure," Alan said. He looked at Lilith. "She needs help with her surfboard."

Lilith looked up at him with a raised brow. "They're like fifteen pounds," she said under her breath.

Alan shrugged and drew her into a walk. Greta had already sauntered ahead, but they soon drew alongside her.

"That's quite the bathing—"

A dog barked three times to their front.

Lilith looked up, scanning the lot. Her eyes landed on Alan's brother, Brad, standing between two cars at the parking lot's edge. His hands drew arcs above his head as if polishing the air.

"Hey, cool," Alan said. He grabbed her hand, pulling her into a jog toward his older brother, leaving Greta to trail in their wake.

Brad flapped a hand toward his chest as they neared, making slight bobs of his head, with a taut jaw and saucer eyes.

"Hey, Brad," Alan said. "What's up?"

"We've got trouble," Brad said. "They're after us."

Lilith paled. She didn't need to hear their name to know who *they* were.

"But how?" Her eyes scanned the lot. People threaded between cars, coming and going. A cluster of three blond-haired surfers chatted to one side. The hand of one drew a sinuous path through the air, dropping the jaws of the others. About fifty feet to the right, Brad's light blue Volkswagen van idled with Lucy at the wheel.

Lilith held up a hand, and Lucy smiled and waved in return. Moments later, a black nose pushed her aside, revealing a furry, mostly white face framed by black. Bear's pink mouth snapped like a camera's shutter as he barked a triple greeting of his own.

"Is that Bear?" Alan asked. "Where did he come from?"

Chapter 7

Lucy

Lucy's head swivelled, searching the parking lot. To facilitate a quick getaway, she'd stopped alongside the row of parked cars closest to the beach rather than in a designated parking spot. All around her, trunks and doors slammed while people slipped between vehicles heading to and from the beach.

She sucked in a breath as taillights flared to her left. A sporty yellow convertible, top down, reversed a step in her direction. The chick driving it made a shooing motion with a hand.

Lucy nodded before edging ahead a few feet.

She stuck out her tongue as the departing vehicle sped past a moment later. "Snooty pants."

Movement in the rear-view mirror yanked her eyes up and to the right. In its reflection, a dark blue Chevy van rolled into view several cars back. Lucy's heart thumped in her chest as it surged toward her bumper.

Slow down, idiot. She rolled ahead a few more feet as the driver swung it toward the beach. With narrowed eyes, she watched the lumbering box pull into the recently vacated spot.

Lucy snorted. *Oh, brother.*

An airbrushed mural covered the van's windowless side. A red dragon stretched from the vehicle's front to the centre of the cargo side door. A heavily muscled chain-mail-armoured man stood opposite it, near the rear, holding a sword in two hands, with his mouth open in a snarl of defiance. A pale and tattooed arm rested on the sill of the vehicle's open passenger-side window. Silver rings adorned the hand of the arm's owner.

Bear growled, nosing the air near her ear.

She glanced at the dog. "Easy, Bear. It's just a couple of headbangers."

Patting his head, she shifted in her seat, feeling pressure near her middle.

Great. She had to pee.

There hadn't been time before fleeing the apartment. After a night's sleep, she wasn't going to last much longer.

Lucy looked toward the restaurant that lay to her front. *Later*, she thought. She grimaced, popped the top button of her jeans, and leaned back in her seat. *I can hold it a bit longer.*

A few people crossed the pavement as she did so. A heavyset woman with a straw hat and floral-print one-piece pinched her nose, giving the van a meaningful scowl as she and two elementary-school-age kids walked past.

Sighing, Lucy killed the engine.

They needed to get out of town first. They could stop at a gas station or restaurant on the way.

It was probably partly nerves anyway. She had more reason than the others to be worried about being caught. The others were American citizens. That probably afforded them some protection from the Bodhi Group, but that didn't include Lucy. As a foreign student, who knew what being caught might mean for her? At best, she might be sent back home to Canada. This close to the school year, there would be no way she'd be able to get into another school in time. She'd miss a year for sure. Her parents would totally freak. The thought scared her as much as the

Bodhi Group.

No, she would have to hold it. If worse came to worst, she'd just pay for car detailing.

On the positive side, the Bodhi Group might not even know who she was. Her name wasn't on the lease for their apartment, and Brad's van was, of course, registered in his name. Not that it made her feel much better. Her concern for her friends matched what she felt for herself.

Her knuckles whitened on the steering wheel. It wasn't fair. They'd done nothing wrong. Unless being attacked by outlaws and helping a fellow traveller get to safety were crimes.

She turned her eyes to the sand.

Come on, guys.

Brad stood with his back to her, between two cars at the parking lot's edge, looking out at the sand. He jumped, waving his hands, and gave a shout.

Bear's bark erupted in her ears a second later. She clapped her hands to the sides of her head, then gave him a look. "Are you trying to deafen me?"

The dog rumbled and regarded her, tilting his head left, then right.

Lucy smiled and squinted an eye. "That look's gotten you out of trouble before, hasn't it?"

She tousled his fur, then returned her gaze to the beach.

Movement along the line of Brad's gaze drew her eyes to Lilith and Alan out on the sand. As Lucy sighted them, the young couple broke into a trot. Alan led, towing Lilith with his left hand, holding a surfboard with his right.

As they neared, Brad stepped out from the cars to meet them, and Alan's lips moved, his words not quite audible. She stuck her head out the window to better hear. A half second later, something warm and furry shoved her aside, pressing her against the window frame. She winced, feeling multiple points of pressure, like dull knitting needles, digging into the denim covering her thighs. Her ears rang a moment later, once again sending a hand to her ear to muffle her canine companion's bark.

"Come *on*, Bear," she said, giving him a push. The weight lifted from her lap as Bear withdrew. Sitting to her right, the dog shot glances between her and the beach. "Settle down. They're coming."

The dog lunged toward her and a moist tongue fluttered against her ear, then drew a trail across her cheek. She squealed, giving the dog another shove, sending Bear back to the passenger seat with an apologetic huff.

Lucy rubbed her face with her shirt.

"God, Bear." She stuck her pinkie into her ear, clearing away saliva. "How'd you like it if I licked you?"

She raised a brow at the dog, who regarded her quizzically.

"What am I saying? Of course you'd love that, wouldn't you?" She shook a finger at him. "No more licking. All right?"

Bear chuffed a sound that might have been agreement. "Good boy."

It was weird, she thought. He was usually quiet and well behaved. *Maybe too much time away from Olivia and Wilhelm.*

She returned her gaze to her friends. Lilith now held the surfboard. Alan stood a few feet from the group, talking to a strange woman in a sky-blue hat and a skimpy swimsuit. The woman said something in reply, then gave a shrug.

Alan backpedalled, mouthing words at Lilith and Brad. The latter two pivoted and strode toward Lucy a moment later while Alan rotated in the opposite direction and sprinted over the sand.

"Where's Alan going?" she asked as Brad slid the van's cargo door aside.

"He's getting his stuff," Brad said, taking the surfboard from Lilith.

"Hey, girlfriend."

"Hi, Lucy." The teen gave a wry smile, climbing into the back and kneeling by the front seats. "What's the plan?"

"Let's wait for Alan," Brad said, his voice coming from beyond the open door.

Lucy grasped Lilith's hand. "Once we get out of town, we'll figure something out."

The two women watched Brad lift Lilith's surfboard over his head. Placing a foot inside the van, he pulled himself up. His head disappeared above the open door. Grunts, slaps and scraping sounds came from the ceiling moments later.

Before long, Brad's head reappeared and he climbed inside, shutting the door after himself. Nudging the hundred pounds of wagging fur occupying the passenger seat out of the way, he settled into place. "Do you see him?"

"Here he comes," Lilith said, pointing.

Holding a long surfboard as if to block rain, Alan skirted the van's front. Tossing a towel and bag inside the back, he hauled himself up the van's side as a screech of tires from the street snapped Lucy's head to the right.

"Oh my god," Lilith said. "Is that them?"

Chapter 8

Alan

Alan craned his neck. Cars continued to drive south down the highway, but northbound traffic sat idle. In the distance, near the intersection, raised arms shook from open car windows. The blare of another horn sounded as traffic on that side began to flow again.

"Nah, looks like someone had a near miss," he said, resuming his work lashing the surfboard to the roof.

Leaping inside, he reached for the door handle, and pulled. The door stopped after a foot as fingers wrapped around its edge. The handle slipped from Alan's grasp as the door reversed direction with unexpected force.

Greta, his would-be surfing student, stood a few feet away. Two pale-skinned and gaunt dudes accompanied her. One held the van's door ajar while the other hovered by the redhead's right shoulder. Both sported tattoos down each bare arm and long dark brown hair running past their shoulders. A black KISS T-shirt clung to the skinny frame of the one holding the door. The other wore a white T-shirt with black sleeves with AC/DC emblazoned across the chest.

The AC/DC fan walked toward the van's front.

"S'up, Greta." Alan spread his hands. "Like I said, I . . . I gotta go."

Greta shot a glance at the wannabe member of the KISS army. "I'm afraid not."

Blocking the door with a hip, the dude pulled something from behind his back. Alan's mouth grew dry, and his insides churned, as he stared down the barrel of a handgun.

"What the fuck?"

"You are leaving," Greta said, "but not without—"

Alan fell back onto his hands as a blur of black and white knocked him aside. The gunman's eyes widened, and he reeled back with a cry as Bear leaped upon him. The dog's head ripped left and right. The gunman's mouth gaped, emitting a shriek, and the clatter of metal against pavement followed. As Alan picked himself up from the van's floor, the hard rocker rained punches against the dog's head, then stumbled back as Bear released him.

As his butt hit the pavement, the dude rolled onto his side, cradled his arm, and whimpered.

Whirling on Greta, Bear growled. Throaty and guttural, it froze her in place with her hands twisted in front of her like claws. Her skin took on a flickering glow, as if lit by firelight.

With the whites of her eyes showing, she slowly lowered her hands.

"Holy shit," said her headbanger companion. He scrabbled away from the enraged canine, heedless of his injured wrist, leaving bloody palm prints on the pavement.

Greta held her hands out before her, keeping her eyes fixed on Bear. "Stand down."

"What?" said a voice coming from Alan's left. Glancing toward it, he saw the other headbanger standing in their path, holding a second handgun pointed in Lucy's direction. "Are you nuts? We've got them dead to rights."

"You heard me, Dennis," Greta said. "Let them go. The situation has changed."

Alan's eyes darted between the scene out the cargo door and the thug that stood beyond the windshield.

"This is bullshit, Greta." Alan sighed in relief as the dude named Dennis sidled to the right and lowered his weapon. "You'd better—" Dennis's face blanched as Bear's head swivelled to face him.

Alan gripped the door handle. "Come on, Bear," he said to the dog's back.

The dog ignored him and instead paced to the left a few steps, all the while keeping his head fixed on the hottie and the headbangers. The dog barked twice more, then flicked his head like a bull preparing to charge.

At this, the trio backed up, then fled into the cluster of parked cars, ducking their heads as they did so.

With a last bark, Bear whirled. The dog dipped his snout, then flicked it up twice, then a third time, giving a short bark.

Alan stepped outside and stood. "Come on, boy."

Bear dodged Alan's hands and ran a few steps to the front of the van. Sitting on his haunches, the dog stared at the VW's windshield. Sunlight reflecting off the dog's retinas gave his eyes a fiery glow.

"What the hell . . ." Alan trailed off.

Lucy's voice rose from within the van. "Get in, Alan. He wants us to go without him."

"No way," Lilith said. She knelt beside Alan. "Come on, Bear. Here, Bear."

The dog rotated his head to the left and right, then again.

Lilith shot Alan a look. "Did he just shake his head no?"

"Yeah," he answered. "Sure looks like it."

"Goddamn it," Lucy yelled, drawing Alan's gaze. Her eyes bored into Alan's through the open cargo door. "Get in the fucking van, you two. Now!"

Alan's jaw dropped. Lucy never swore . . . or raised her voice. He had always figured it was a Canadian thing or something.

He put a foot on the door's edge, preparing to follow Lilith, who had already leaped inside, and hesitated. "But, Luce," he said. "We can't just leave him."

Lucy inhaled sharply, then exhaled like a punctured tire. "He wants us to go without him. Please . . . just get in. He'll be fine."

"Do it, Alan," Brad said. "Lucy's right. He tracked us all the way from Dublin Gulch. He'll find us again."

Alan grunted and climbed inside. "You dudes better be right." He pulled the door shut. "You don't leave a man behind."

He braced himself against the back seat as the vehicle lurched into motion.

"It's what he wanted," Lucy said. "I know it."

He felt Lilith's hand under an armpit as she helped him onto the back seat, where he settled in beside her.

When he looked out the side window again, he could see no sign of Bear.

"Yeah?" Alan scowled at the back of Lucy's head. "What makes you so sure?"

Lucy met Alan's gaze in the rear-view mirror. "Because . . . he told me so."

Chapter 9

Lucy

Lucy looked back out the window, feeling a rush of blood to her cheeks. No one said anything for several heartbeats as she steered the van through the maze of parked cars before exiting onto the highway that ran parallel to the beach. She kept to the speed limit but watched the rear-view mirror for any signs of pursuit. She saw none.

"Excuse me?" Alan said. "He told you?"

"I got that too," Brad said. "He kept moving his head like he was telling us to get moving."

But it was more than that. She'd heard him, felt his presence inside her head as the dog stared into her eyes.

They'd connected . . . somehow.

He hadn't communicated with words, though. It wasn't a conversation in the traditional sense, but more an exchange of understanding. Their eyes had met, and she'd simply had a sudden realization of the dog's desires, mixed with a sense of urgency. He wanted them to run. He'd make sure they got away.

It wasn't scary exactly, but it still freaked her out.

Except, now that it was over, it felt ridiculous. She should have just left it at a feeling, not said that Bear had *literally* told her. *They must think I'm crazy.* She just hadn't known what else to do. Alan had been so insistent that they not leave Bear behind, she hadn't known what else to say to convince him. She hadn't meant to swear at Alan, either. It was as if Bear's agitation had lit a spark inside of her.

"I . . . I don't know how to explain it," Lucy said, studying the road. "We had some kind of connection, and I just knew he wanted us to run and that'd he'd make sure we got away."

"You just knew?" Alan said. "Like telepathy?"

Lucy shrugged. "Yeah, I guess so."

"Huh," Brad said. "I guess we knew he wasn't an ordinary pooch. I mean, he belongs to a couple of gods."

Lucy glanced right. "I don't think he belongs to them."

"What, like he's been stolen?" Lilith asked.

Lucy pressed the brake as the light at the approaching intersection turned red. "I don't think he belongs to anyone. I just got this sense that he's his own . . . dog."

"Forget about that," Alan said. "Who were those guys?"

"Must be the Bodhi Group," Lucy replied.

"I don't think so," Brad said. "They weren't dressed like agents."

The van tilted as Lucy turned another corner.

"They could be undercover, though, right?" Lilith said. "I mean even if that Greta . . . person . . . was practically naked. I totally had a bad feeling the moment I saw her."

"Whoever they were," Lucy said, "the plan hasn't changed. We've got to get out of town."

"But to where?" Lilith asked,

"How about Big Sur?" Alan said. "If we're going to be hiding out, we might as well do it somewhere we can surf."

"Maybe," Brad said. "North is as good a direction as any. We can stop in LA for supplies."

"We've got to stop before then." Lucy studied the buildings by the roadside. "I need a washroom."

"Me too." Brad leaned left to glance at the fuel gauge. "Looks like we need gas anyway."

"Are you guys crazy?" Lilith asked. "They'll catch us."

"No choice." Brad turned in his seat. "The tank's almost empty. Big Sur's hours away."

"And I've *really* got to go," Lucy added.

"Besides," Brad said, "I think they've got bigger problems. Like a pissed-off Alaskan shepherd on their tail."

Lilith giggled. "I hope he's okay."

Lucy nodded. "Me too."

No one said anything for a while after that.

Before long, they pulled into a gas station near the edge of town. Lucy pulled the keys from the ignition, jumped to the asphalt, and hustled inside the building.

"Washroom's at the side, miss," said the grizzled old guy behind the counter, pointing over his shoulder. He handed her a hubcap with a key attached by a twist of wire. "Be sure to bring back the—"

The rest was lost as the door closed behind her.

Lucy raised the hubcap to Brad as she exited and jogged to the side of the building. Five minutes later, she dried her hands with a paper towel, used it to turn the doorknob, and nudged the door wide with her foot.

"Much better," she said, holding the key out to Brad, who stood waiting outside.

"Thanks, babe," he said, taking the key.

Lucy passed Alan standing by the van's rear as he returned the fuel hose to the side of the pump. She pulled open the driver's door and reached inside to retrieve her purse. Lilith sat inside, eating from a bag of chips. The girl waved a greeting, then popped a chip into her mouth and crunched, making faint humming sounds as she did so. Lucy smiled, closed the driver's-side door, and went inside to get snacks of her own.

Within ten minutes, the VW bus rumbled to life as Brad turned the key. Lucy settled into the passenger seat and sucked Coke from a can through a red-and-white straw.

"All right," Brad said, putting the vehicle into gear. "Let's move."

He swung the car left and turned onto the road.

Lucy swallowed, enjoying the liquid's tickle as it made its way down her throat. "You should probably call your parents when we get to LA."

"What are you going to tell them, Brad?" Alan asked.

"I don't know," Brad said, glancing at the rear-view mirror. "I guess that we all decided to take one last trip."

"Just don't tell them where we're going," Lucy said. "Their phone might be bugged, or they might tell the wrong person."

"Paranoid much?" Lilith said.

Lucy turned to face the rear and smiled. "Better safe than sorry."

Lilith bobbed her head. "No, you're right."

"Are we going to Big Sur, then?" Alan asked with a smile.

Brad shrugged, keeping his eyes on the road. "It's as good a place as any, I suppose. That or we keep driving until we hit Canada." He looked at Lucy. "Think your parents will mind some unannounced visitors?"

Lucy snorted. "Are you kidding? They'd love the chance to finally meet you." She paused. "They're probably at the lake. They usually spend all summer there."

Movement in the side mirror drew Lucy's eye to the right.

"Oh, yeah," Lilith said, "your summer's like super short, isn't it?"

Lucy sat upright and twisted in her seat. Her mouth dropped open, and she bugged her eyes.

Seconds later, Bear, the Alaskan shepherd, shot her a glance as he sped past the moving van. Racing ahead twenty feet, he turned his head left and barked.

"Holy shit," Brad said. "Told you he'd find us."

The van slowed and swung right toward the shoulder.

Lucy called to Bear as the vehicle rolled to a stop.

The dog shook his head, barked, and trotted ahead a few feet, then looked back.

Lucy looked at Brad with wide eyes. "Follow him."

No sooner had the van begun to creep forward than Bear trotted away, picking up speed with each step. Before long, the dog's legs blurred, and his paws pounded the pavement.

"How fast are we going?" Lucy asked.

"About forty-five," Brad replied. "I didn't think dogs could run this fast."

"What about greyhounds?" said Lilith's voice from the rear.

"Maybe," Brad said. "I don't think they can keep it up for long."

"Yeah," Alan said, "but Bear's no Greyhound."

Lucy smirked. "No, he isn't . . . he's something better."

Their canine guide slowed to turn onto a side street. He picked up speed again before making another turn. The van's engine revved, labouring to keep up, as its occupants wobbled in their seats. Occasionally, the dog would glance back, then take off even faster.

"I wonder where he's taking us," Lucy said.

Brad shot her a glance. "Beats me." He looked left and right. "We're heading roughly southwest."

"Isn't that back the way we came?" She hadn't grown up around here like Brad and had yet to visit much of the area. For all she knew, they'd already left town and entered the boundaries of another. This close to Los Angeles, towns merged into one another without a break, unlike back home, where hundreds of miles of rolling green or snowy fields separated them.

"Kind of," Brad said. He stabbed a finger past her face. "We're up the coast from the pier, though."

Lucy's forehead creased. "Oh, great."

Brad looked at her sidelong. "Don't worry. If we stay off the main streets, we should be fine. What are the odds that they'd choose the same random side street? They don't even know which direction we went."

"Yeah, I suppose so." Her forehead smoothed, and she nodded, deciding what he said was true until proven otherwise. There was no sense worrying about it. Besides, her recent connection with her furry friend gave her faith that Bear wouldn't lead them into danger.

Brad spun the steering wheel to the right, taking them down another side street.

"Hey," Lilith called from the rear. "This is my street."

Chapter 10

Brad

They drove a few more blocks down a four-car-wide residential street lined with thirty-foot palm trees on either side. *Oh, yeah,* he thought. It had been dark when they'd dropped Lilith off the night before, but he recognized the street now. In the light of day, it looked more like it had weeks ago, when they'd picked her up at the start of the road trip. He snorted to himself. They had had no idea of the adventure and trouble that awaited them. *If I knew then what I know now . . .*

"My house is just up here," Lilith said. "On the right."

"Weird," Alan added. "How does he know where you live?"

Lucy turned in her seat. "More importantly, why is he taking us there?"

Their canine guide slowed to a trot, sniffing the air.

"Maybe he isn't," Brad said. "It could be a coincidence." He flicked his eyes to Lucy for confirmation.

She tossed her shoulders. "Doesn't seem likely, but I guess we'll see."

Fifty feet later, the dog stopped next to a dark BMW coupe. Brad steered front first into the empty spot behind it. The weight of a hand pulled against his seat as he snugged the Microbus against the curb.

"That's my house," Lilith said, pointing a finger past Brad's ear.

She pointed to a well-maintained tan two-storey house. It sat on a narrow plot of land, enclosed by a solid four-foot-high stone fence. Plants of various types grew within the foot-wide garden that fronted the stucco-covered wall. A wrought-iron gate near the fence's centre provided access to a stone-paved courtyard, within which comfortable outdoor furniture sat beneath broad umbrellas.

"Perfect," Brad said. "You can let your parents know you're going to be away."

"Maybe you shouldn't," Lucy said. "I mean . . . if they say no, what do we do then?"

Lilith wagged her head. "Nah, it'll be okay. School's not for a few weeks, and I think they're enjoying having some time alone together. It'll be fine."

Lucy glanced out the front. "That's if Bear doesn't take off again," she said, pointing out the window.

The dog sat in the street, next to the 3 Series BMW, and gazed inside. The lone occupant, visible through the rear window, sat reclined in the driver's seat. A thatch of brown hair sprouted from the edges of the taupe bucket hat that covered his face.

Bear tapped the door with a paw and gave a low woof.

The driver twitched upright, and his arms flapped.

After a moment, the car door swung open, and a man of average build and height emerged. His hairy arms stretched skyward from short sleeves, and his mouth gaped.

Kneeling, he tousled the dog's fur, earning a few wet licks in return, then fired a look at the VW van. Ice-blue eyes studied Brad a moment, then flicked to his companions.

Standing, the man placed his hat back atop his head, adjusted it, then walked over.

"You must be Brad," the stranger said in a smooth

baritone. The lines on his tanned face deepened as the corners of his mouth rose. The salt-and-pepper three-day beard put his age somewhere in the forties or early fifties. He extended a hand through the open window. "Glad to meet you. Name's Carver." Brad clasped the offered hand automatically, mouth ajar. Carver's grip was strong, his palm dry. He looked past Brad. "You must be Lucy." He leaned right to peer into the back. "Which makes that Alan and Lilith." His gaze returned to Brad and his face contorted into a yawn. "Oh, sorry about that." He looked down at Bear, who sat at his side, looking up at the two of them. "I didn't get much sleep last night. Thanks to this guy."

"Who are you, man?" Brad asked. "How do you know our names?"

Carver's chin retreated and an eyebrow rose. "Like I said, it's Carver. Carver MacReady. As for how I know your names"—he glanced down at the Alaskan shepherd—"Bear told me, of course."

Brad looked at Carver sidelong. "No, really. Are you with the Bodhi Group or something?"

Carver's eyebrows jumped. "No." He looked around. "It's just me." He paused and looked down, holding a finger to his ear.

Brad's head swivelled to regard the others. Alan and Lilith crouched by the front seats, mouths open, while Lucy chewed her bottom lip. Apparently noticing Brad's gaze, she shrugged and turned her palms to the ceiling.

"Trust me," Carver said as Brad turned back to face him. "I'm not with them. I'm here to get you somewhere safe." He looked up and down the street. "We should get going. Trouble could show up at any moment. Just follow me. We've got a bit of a drive ahead of us." He leaned in and looked at the van's dashboard. "You all topped up?"

Brad snorted. "Look, man."

"Carver."

"Sure . . . Carver. Whatever your name is, there's no way we're following you anywhere until we know more than you've told us. So far, you haven't told us . . . shit. If Bear didn't seem to trust you—"

"All right," Carver said, holding up a hand. "All right. Like I said, my name's Carver MacReady. I'm a private investigator."

"Like *Magnum PI?*" Lilith asked.

Carver flashed white teeth, then chuckled. "Yeah, sure. Something like that."

"Cool," Lilith said.

"Anyway," Carver continued, "I sometimes do work for the Schmidts. First names Wilhelm, and Olivia. I believe you know them. Judging by your faces, you definitely do know them . . . not that I doubted it." He glanced around once more, then leaned in closer. "Late last night, or early this morning, depending on how you look at it, this ball of fur wakes me out of a dead sleep, barking down my door. He needs my help, he tells me. Some kids that are important to the Schmidts are in trouble. Before long, I'm driving down from LA with him." Carver pointed a finger at Lilith's house. "He led me here, then told me to watch that house and ran off. I guess I fell asleep at some point because next thing I know, here you are."

"What do you mean, he told you?" Lucy said. "Dogs don't talk."

Carver tapped his index finger against his temple. "He doesn't need to talk. When he wants me to know something, I suddenly just know it. It's spooky at first, but you get used to it. It sounds nuts, I know, but if you know the Schmidts, you know this is the least of the weird shit that surrounds them."

Brad jabbed a thumb toward the windshield. "How does a PI afford a car like that?"

"The Schmidts pay very well." Carver glanced over Brad's shoulder. "I guess you could say they're like my Robin Masters, except that's *my* car, not just a loaner." His eyes flicked over the group. "Satisfied?"

Brad nodded as the others mumbled their agreement.

"Good." Carver slapped the windowsill. "We should get going, then."

"Where are we headed?" Brad asked.

"Los Angeles," Carver said. "To a safe house there."

"For how long?"

Carver shrugged. "Until whoever is after you gives up or is no longer a threat, I suppose. Sorry I can't be more specific. We'll have to wait for Wilhelm or Olivia to contact us after you're safe."

Bear barked, drawing Carver's eyes down. "Right. We should move."

"Wait," Lilith cried. "I should tell my mom."

"Go for it," Carver said, "but be quick."

"Yuck," Lilith said. "There's that homely bird again."

"What bird?" Brad asked, following her gaze.

A turkey vulture, half again the size of a house cat, sat atop a fence across and down the street.

Alan's head appeared next to Brad's as he leaned to look. "Oh, yeah. I keep seeing those things. I saw one at the pier this morning, too."

Bear turned at Alan's words and growled lowly as Carver whirled. Crouching into a shooter's stance, the PI drew a pistol from the small of his back and pulled the trigger. The muzzle flashed but made almost no sound.

"Dammit," Carver said as the bird took flight toward them before veering away.

"Is he shooting at it?" Lilith hissed.

Carver fired several more times until the bird twitched and dropped. It careened across the terracotta shingles of a nearby house, wings flapping, before disappearing over the roof's peak.

"What the hell, dude?" Brad said, white-knuckling the steering wheel. "It's just a bird."

"Sir Bear doesn't think so," Carver said, eyes fixed on the rooftop across the street. He turned to face the van. "We've got to go. I winged it, but there may be more around." He looked over Brad's shoulder. "Forget about telling your parents. You can call them from the safe house."

"Okay," Lilith said in a low tone, "but why did you kill that bird? It was ugly, but I didn't want—"

"It would've followed us . . . and it'll survive . . . probably."

"What makes you so sure?" Alan asked.

"The enemy's spies are resilient." Carver knelt and smoothed the fur between Bear's ears. The dog woofed. Carver laughed as a pink tongue slapped across a cheek. Still chuckling, he straightened. "Bear's riding with you." He sidled toward the BMW, still talking. "Follow me. I'll lead the way."

Brad returned the PI's two-fingered salute and twisted the key while Alan opened the cargo door, letting in their canine friend. Putting the VW bus into gear, he swung out and followed the PI's car.

The top of Bear's head appeared next to Brad's hand as he switched gears. Putting it into second, he gave Bear's head a pat, earning a lick on the wrist before the dog withdrew.

It felt good to be moving again. He tilted his head back and swirled it clockwise, then counter-clockwise. Inhaling a lungful of air, he expelled it as if it were his last, feeling the knots in his neck untie.

The gun had freaked him out. The weapon's near-total lack of sound somehow made it worse. *Must have been a silencer*, he thought. He hadn't seen the characteristic screw-on cylinder, but he wasn't a gun guy. *Who knows what other options might be available?*

A silent weapon struck Brad as a killer's tool, and that made him nervous. *Not to mention the dude's a total stranger. Well, not totally.* The man clearly knew, or at least knew of, Wilhelm and Olivia. But that didn't make him trustworthy either. *Knowing someone doesn't make you a friend.*

That Carver clearly liked dogs—or at least Bear—Brad took as a good sign. *With a soft spot for animals, how bad can he be?* That suggested they probably weren't dealing with a psycho. He'd read somewhere that psychopaths could be charming, though, so that also wasn't enough on its own.

No, there were only two solid reasons to trust Carver that Brad could see. The first was that Bear had led them here, and clearly the pooch liked the dude. The second, and the clincher, was that if Carver wanted to hurt or kidnap them, he had had the means and opportunity to do so but had done neither.

Brad cranked the steering wheel right, then pressed the accelerator.

No, Carver seemed legit, and following him seemed their best bet, at least for now.

"What did that Carver dude mean?" Alan said.

"About what?" Brad asked.

"About the bird following us . . . why would it follow us? And . . . why would it matter?"

Brad glanced sidelong at Lucy. "I don't know . . . but if Bear can talk to Carver . . . maybe that turkey vulture can talk to whoever is after us."

"Oh, great," Lilith said. "Now we can't even trust

animals." Bear gave a yap. "Sorry, boy. Of course we trust *you*."

Brad snorted and shook his head. A warm hand grasped his own.

"You okay, sweetie?" Lucy said.

Brad nodded. "Yeah ... I guess so ... just thinking. Talking dogs, spying birds. What's next?"

Chapter 11

Greta

Greta knelt to examine the bird, which opened an eye to regard her. The injured wing already showed signs of healing. They would have to take it with them. A good meal would provide it the fuel that it needed to fully restore itself and join its brethren in the hunt. With luck, their spies would reacquire the youths before long. In the meantime, she and her companions would make their way to the LA stronghold to wait for that moment. As the closest major city, she judged it probable that they'd head there first.

She pointed to Dennis, the taller of her two companions. "Help the bird into the van. It's coming with us." She looked at the other one. *Carl? No, Cole.* "My clothes?"

Cole stuck his bandaged hand at the head of the dragon decorating the van's side. "In the back."

"Get them for me, please." She ran her hands across her buttocks. "I can feel the sunburn already."

"Sorry, Greta," replied her companion, handing her a bundle of clothes. "The girl at the shop said it would have all the boys drooling, and she wasn't wrong. That kid's got to be dying of dehydration."

He was right. The bikini had done its job; the teen had been quite ready to follow her, a total stranger, to her waiting companions. That would have been quite satisfactory, but when the girlfriend had shown up, Greta could hardly believe her good fortune. Within another few minutes, her two companions would have tossed them both in the back of their ridiculous van, and they would have been on their way.

"Nonetheless," she said, standing on a foot and shoving the other through a leg of her pants, "I think next time we go for one of the women first and you can wear it."

Cole snickered. "No one wants to see that."

"Why'd you call us off?" said Dennis from the open door at the back of the van. "We had them dead to rights."

Her mouth straightened into a tight line. Then again, she could have had all four, if not for the Anemoi's canine.

"If only thinking it made it so," Greta replied, pulling on a T-shirt. She flipped her hands near her ears, spilling red hair down to her shoulders. "I told you. The shepherd is not to be trifled with." She hadn't expected a knight to be protecting pawns, and she hadn't survived this long by being reckless. She dared not challenge the canine without more than these two to back her up. "Count yourselves lucky not to be pushing boulders in Hades right now."

Grabbing the kids, who had been spotted in Shivurr's company near Dublin Gulch by one of their feathered spies, had seemed like the right move, following his escape. Once taken, they would soon be made to reveal all they knew about where the Allfrost Sentinel had gone. Though he had foiled her kidnapping attempt, the dog's presence at least confirmed the youths' value to the opposition. In which case whatever remained after their interrogations could be used as bait or for an exchange.

The corners of her mouth rose. Even if they knew nothing, it would still be a win for her, moving her a step closer to ascension.

She'd been so close, though. Her jaw flexed and blood rushed to her cheeks. *So close.*

Sparks of azure and alabaster rose from her bracelets and enveloped her fists before arcing downward to melt holes in the asphalt. She blew out a breath, slackening her grip, and the crackling light, still blinding in daylight, faded and died.

She had been taken by surprise.

It would not happen again.

Author's Note

I hope you've enjoyed hanging out again with Shivurr's Californian friends and the Schmidts' mysterious dog, Bear. Clearly the gang's adventures in Shivurr's world are far from over.

If you're looking for more, you can find links to other books in the *Phantom Frost* series on alfredwurr.com.

The Shepherd takes place just after the events of *Phantom Frost*, book one in the series, so book two, *Frost God Rising*, is the best one to read next.

However, if you haven't yet, I recommend first reading *Fire Demon Dawn* (a side story featuring Bodhi Institute Security Director Harland Dixon), and, of course, *Phantom Frost*.

Acknowledgements

Special thanks to my wife, Lorelei Pierce, for beta reading the book.

Editing by Clio Editing Services.

About the Author

An avid fan of science fiction and fantasy, be it in movies, books, video games, or RPGs, Alfred has also been, and in many cases continues to be, an Olympic freestyle wrestler (winning national and international championships), a computer scientist (M.Sc.), a software developer and consultant, and a video game developer.

He lives with his wife, Lorelei, in Canada, where staying frosty comes easy half the year.

Subscribe to Alfred's mailing list to get news, updates, and more at: alfredwurr.com/subscribe. You may also contact the author at: alfredwurr.com/contact-page.